18559

King of the Wind

AN INNKEEPER'S HORSE

cover art by Stephen Moore

from KING OF THE WIND by Marguerite Henry

excerpted and adapted by Catherine Nichols

illustrated by Cindy Spenser

designed by Carol Dietz

CHILDRENS PRESS CHOICE

A Checkerboard Press/Macmillan title selected for educational distribution

ISBN 0-516-09601-X

For the first time since he left Morocco, Agba felt safe. He and his beloved Arabian stallion had sailed across the ocean when Sham had been chosen by the sultan as a gift for the king of France. Rejected by the king, Sham had become a cart horse, mistreated and beaten by his cruel owner. Until—and here Agba cast a grateful glance upon his companion—the English Quaker Jethro Coke had stepped in, bought Sham, and offered Agba, along with his cat Grimalkin, a home in England.

"Look," said Mister Coke. "There's Mistress Cockburn, my housekeeper, waiting for us."

A few days later Mister Coke called to his son-in-law, Benjamin Biggle. "Come with me, Benjamin. I've a surprise for thee."

Benjamin peered expectantly into the barn where Agba was gently grooming Sham's still bruised body. "A horse!" he exclaimed. "But Papa Coke, I have never sat a horse." He glanced sidelong at Sham, who twitched his ears in warning.

"We'll wait until spring for your first ride," Mister Coke said. "Let the poor beast recover his strength."

Benjamin sighed. Spring was a long time away.

As the months passed, Sham lost his starveling look. His muscles grew strong and firm. His coat gleamed like burnished gold.

Under the kind mothering of Mistress Cockburn, Agba thrived too. She filled his plate with pigeon pie and dumplings and baked him something sweet each day. From her chatter Agba learned a number of English words, like *eat, poor boy, a bit a cake, kind Mister Coke, fat dolt of a son-in-law*. In return, Agba would open his gold silk bag and show his kind friend the contents—charms against evil and Sham's pedigree.

The day appointed for Benjamin's first ride arrived—a rainy day in early spring. As Sham was being led to the mounting block, he shied, frightened by Benjamin's flapping clothing. Shaking with fear, Benjamin took the reins and tried to thrust his left foot into the stirrup. Instead, he accidentally gave Sham a vicious jab in the ribs.

Quickly, Sham spun around, knocked Benjamin's hat off, and sunk his teeth into his black wig. With a snort of distaste, Sham dropped the wig onto the rain-soaked path.

Benjamin was furious. "I'll ride the beast if it kills me," he muttered. Clapping his wig on his head, he swung one leg over Sham's back, heaved himself into the saddle, and grabbed the reins up short.

Sham sped to the safety of his stall. As he dashed through the door, Benjamin was scraped off his back and into a mud puddle. Then Grimalkin pounced on his head, screamed in his face, and ruined what was left of the wig.

That afternoon, Mister Coke appeared in the barn doorway. "Thou must try to understand, lad," he said. "What happened this morning left my son-in-law very sore." For an instant, his eyes twinkled. "He wishes the horse sent away at once. And my daughter agrees."

Seeing the fright in Agba's eyes, he quickly added, "Come, come, lad. I am merely selling him to Roger Williams, keeper of the Red Lion Inn—a kindly man. He has promised a home above the stable for thee and thy cat."

The innkeeper at the Red Lion *was* kind. His wife, however, hated Agba on sight.

"That varmint-in-a-hood!" she'd shriek. "He gives me the creeps! Get him out of here!" As for Grimalkin, the poor cat couldn't even cross her path without sending her into a fit. One night she accidentally stepped on his tail, causing such a yowling that she insisted both Agba and the cat must leave at once.

Mister Williams walked as far as the road with Agba. "You head back to Jethro Coke now. He'll take you in. I'll look after your horse, I promise."

The innkeeper meant well, but he was abrupt and clumsy. When he saddled Sham the back hairs pulled the wrong way. This made having someone on his back so painful that Sham would toss the rider off.

Mister Williams called in Silas Slade, the best horse-breaker in London. As soon as Mister Slade arrived, he grabbed the reins. He swung up. The next thing he knew a doctor was bending over him, shaking his head.

"I'll break the brute yet!" Slade vowed through swollen lips. "Move him to a small windowless stall," he told Mr. Williams. "Tie him so he can't move. Give him no grain and scarcely any water."

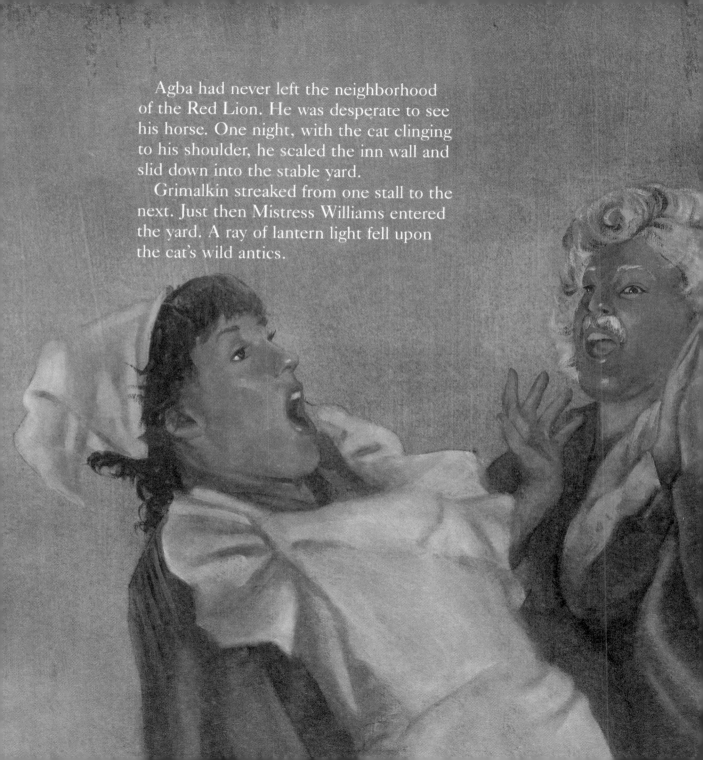

Agba had never left the neighborhood of the Red Lion. He was desperate to see his horse. One night, with the cat clinging to his shoulder, he scaled the inn wall and slid down into the stable yard.

Grimalkin streaked from one stall to the next. Just then Mistress Williams entered the yard. A ray of lantern light fell upon the cat's wild antics.

At the sound of her screeching, everyone in the inn, including the constable, dashed into the yard. Mistress Williams pointed her finger at Agba. "He's a horse thief, constable," she yelled. "Jail him, I beg you!"

Almost before he knew it, the gates of Newgate Prison were clanging shut behind Agba. He was searched. The gold silk bag was found and Sham's pedigree destroyed. Leg irons were clamped about his ankles. He was shoved into a dark, filthy dungeon. His only consolation was Grimalkin.

RED LION INN

Several weeks later Mistress Cockburn decided to visit Agba. Packing a basket brimful of goodies, she took a short coach ride to the Red Lion Inn. She went inside.

A few moments later, she found herself swept out the door by a large, coarse woman yelling, "You'll find the thief in Newgate, you will!"

Mistress Cockburn was so dazed that a coach-and-six almost ran into her. A woman's head looked out the coach window. "For your welfare, madam, I pray you step back out of the lane."

"Begging your pardon," Mistress Cockburn replied, "but the honestest lad I know has been sent to Newgate Prison, and I am all a-twitter."

A gentleman stepped out of the carriage. "I am the earl of Godolphin," he said. "This is my mother-in-law, the dowager duchess of Marlborough. We are on our way to Newgate and would be pleased to have your company."

Flushed with pleasure, Mistress Cockburn gratefully accepted.

Huddled on his skimpy bed of straw, Agba tried to sleep. If he slept he might dream. Then the prison walls would fall away, and he and Sham would be together again.

The door to the dungeon was opening. For a few seconds, Agba was blinded by the light. Then his eyes widened. There stood Mistress Cockburn, tears flowing down her cheeks. "It's him all right!" she exclaimed. "Oh, my poor boy."

Such a warmth and happiness coursed through Agba's body that he feared he would cry too.

"And they call this boy a thief!" Mistress Cockburn was in a rage. "When he only wanted to see his horse which he brought all the way from Morocco."

The duchess turned to her son-in-law. "Perhaps we could help?"

The earl nodded. "Of course. He can come work in my stables at Gog Magog." Agba looked up quickly, a question in his eyes. The earl chuckled. "Don't worry," he said. "We'll go at once to the Red Lion and buy your horse. He will be welcome at Gog Magog. And the cat, too. There is room for all."

Sham lay in his stall at the Red Lion. No one feared him anymore. He was too weak to kick and charge. For weeks he had lived in a kind of daze, indifferent to the smells and sounds of the world around him.

Suddenly, the door of his stall was thrown open, and a boy's slim brown fingers were stroking his neck. An excited whicker escaped him. He lipped the boy. He swiped his cheek with his great pink tongue. Then he neighed his happiness to the whole wide world.

Almost at once Sham struggled to his feet, snorting as if to say, "Let's be off! Somewhere. *Anywhere!*"

In no time at all Agba and Grimalkin were mounted on Sham's back. With the coach-and-six in front, the strange procession wended its slow way to the earl's beautiful estate, Gog Magog.

In his heart Agba knew that the three of them—boy, horse, and cat—had come home at last.